FLYING EYE BOOKS

Magali Bardos

100
BEARS

For my dad, Claude.

1 forest

2 mountains

3 bears on each mountain

4 paws in the air

Eating honey,
5 times a day

6 bears in the forest

7 mushrooms

8 hunters

9 gunshots

10 butterflies flutter by…
the bears seize the chance to sneak away

The clock strikes
11 at night

12 mice tremble

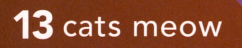

13 cats meow

14 smoking chimneys

On the **15**TH floor

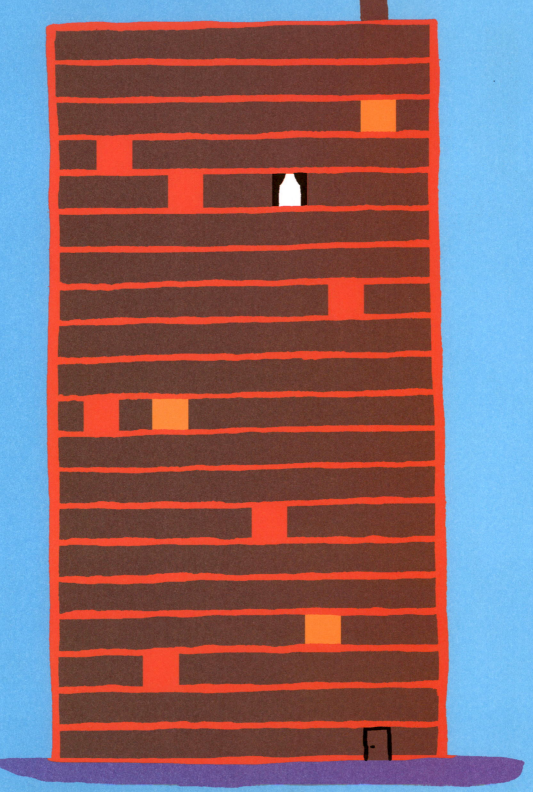

19 hot potatoes

20 desserts to finish

The bears invite themselves to the feast
by climbing up **21** ladder rungs

Suddenly, a mad-house of **22**

23 chairs knocked over

They use **24** balloons to escape

Flying over
route **25**

26 ears

27 cabbages

28 leaves of clover

29 snails

The next day, the bears put on their Sunday bests: **30** buttons well buttoned

To go and celebrate the

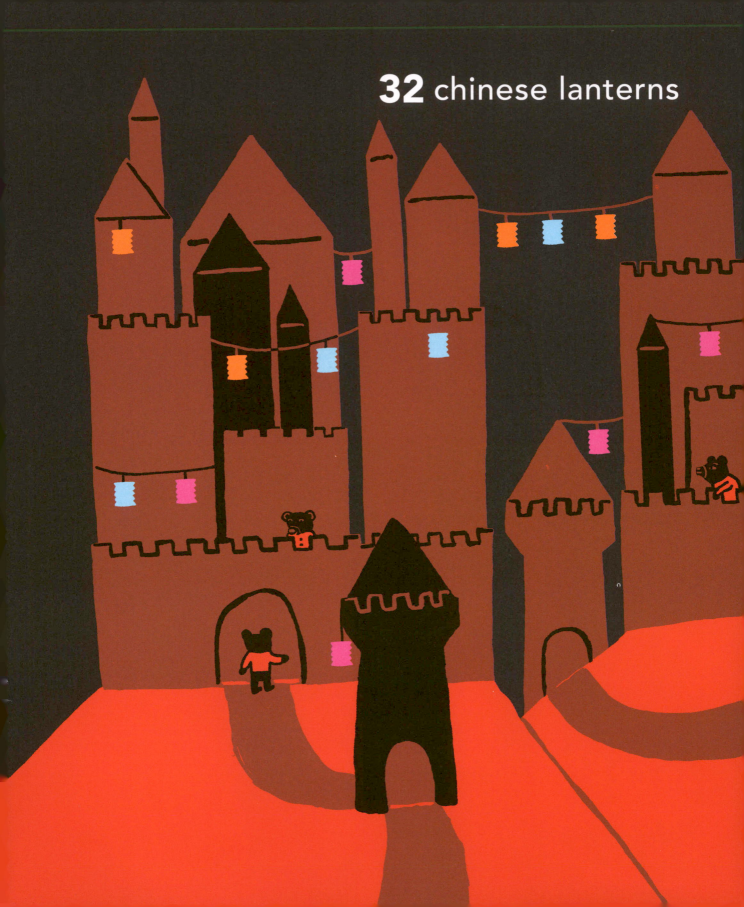

32 chinese lanterns

33 towers

34 steps forward

35 steps backward

36
streamers

37 or **38** bits of confetti...
give or take

But the next day, fevers of **39**°C

40 spoonfuls
of syrup

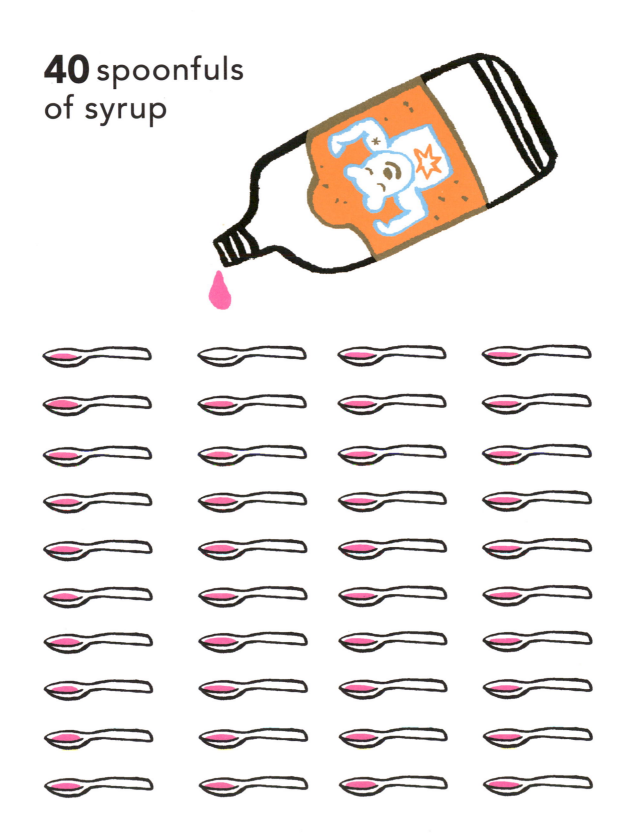

Once they've recovered,
off they go
to number
41

43 lights

44 tiles

45 costumes

46 reserved seats

47 flowers in bouquets

48 bow ties

50 on stage!

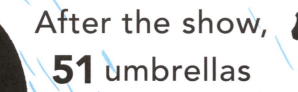

After the show,
51 umbrellas

52 shoes

The bears go
on holiday
in the sun

There are **54** of them in the photos

They meet **55** animals
in the savannah

Further on,
56 exotic fruits
and **57** termites

58 insects altogether!

Masks as souvenirs:
59 circles, **60** feathers
and **61** triangles

62 windows
on the way home

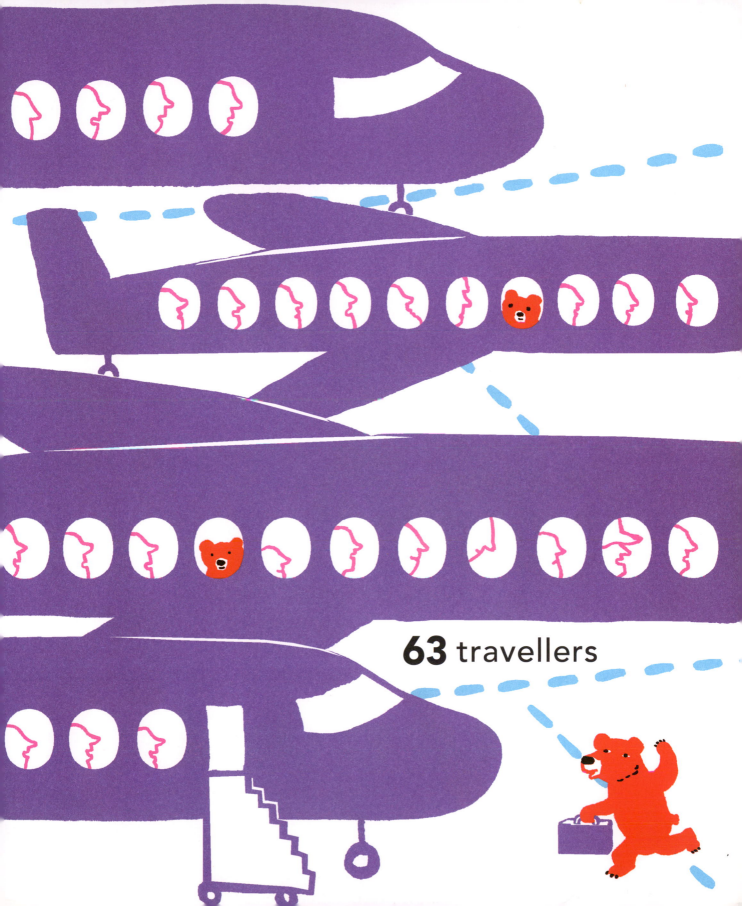

63 travellers

64 objects found at the airport

The **65**TH one
is hidden

The bears arrive back
home at night.

66 eyes

67 stars

But **68** figures all in all!

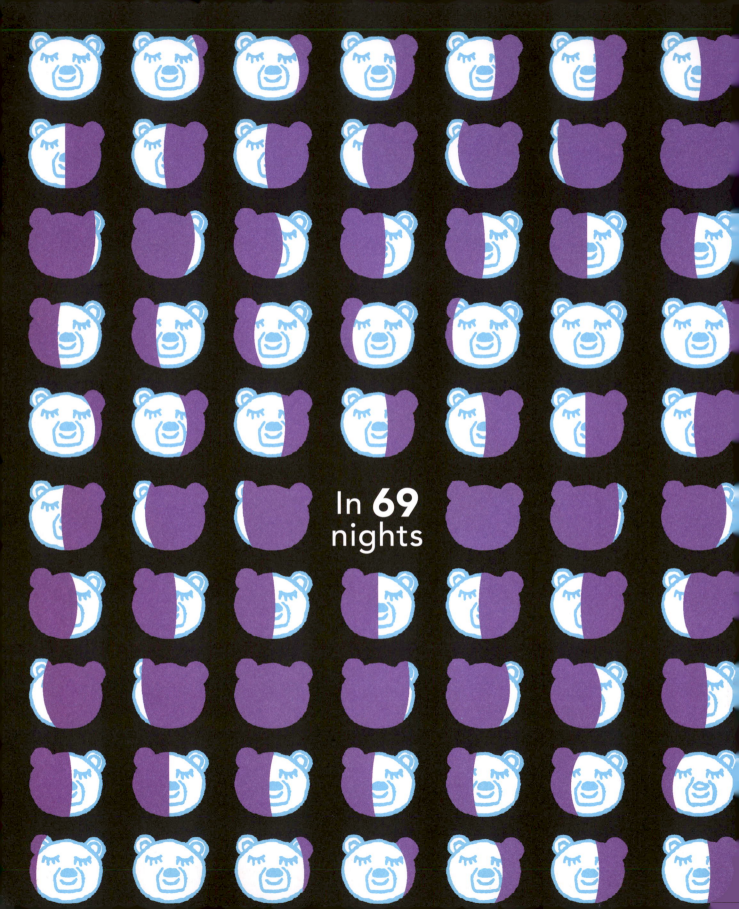

In **69** nights

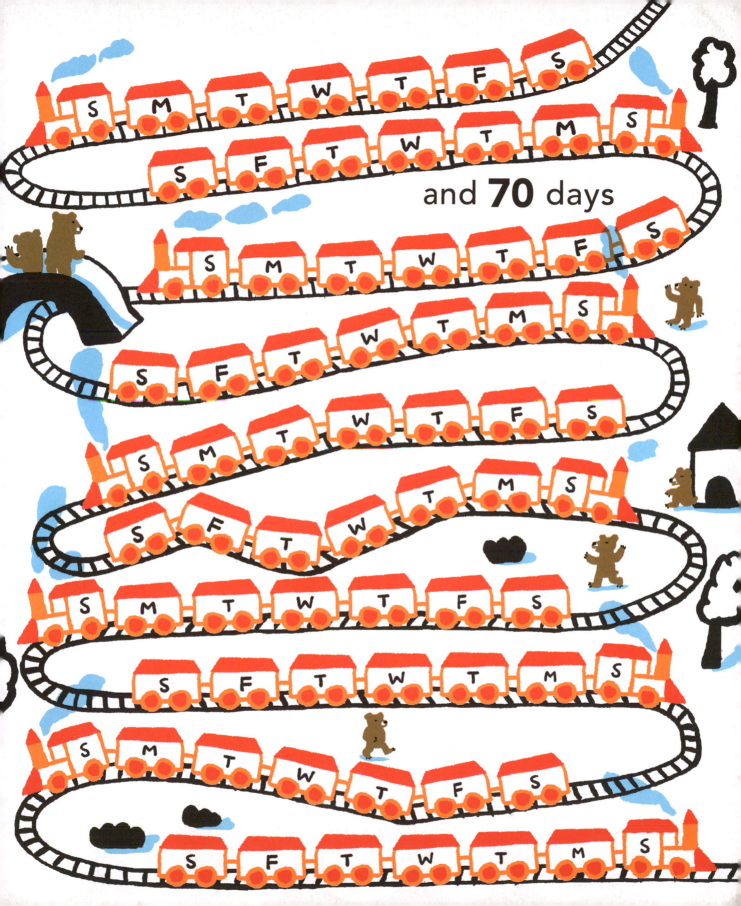

and **70** days

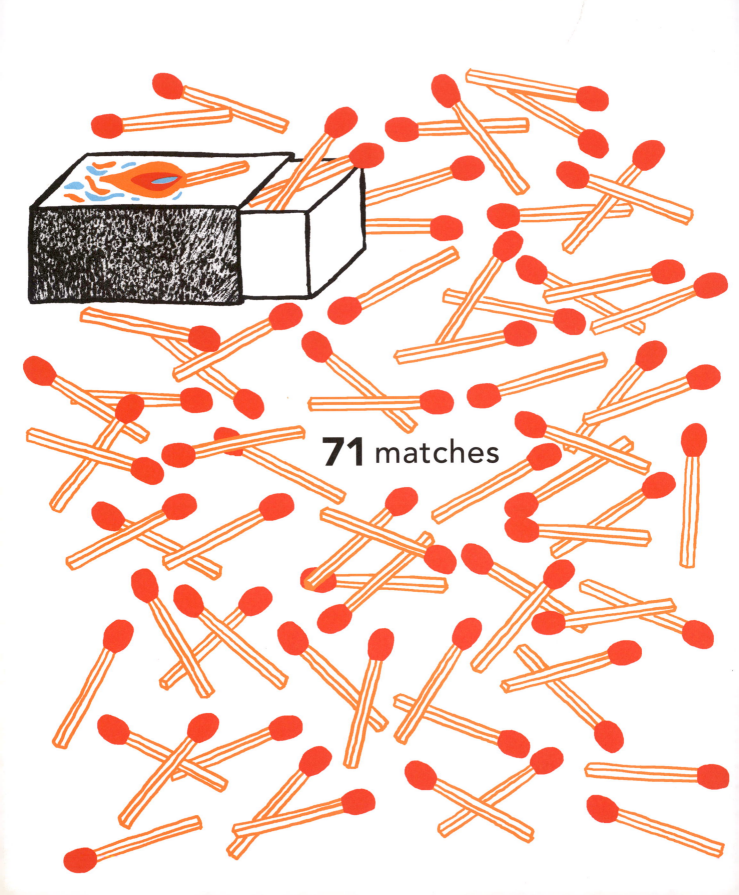

71 matches

73 diamond shapes

74 colouring pencils

It's a party!
75 pieces of the puzzle
and **76** marbles
and balls

77 pins and

78 dots on the dice

Meanwhile, the hunters
are busy fishing…

79 fish

80 toes

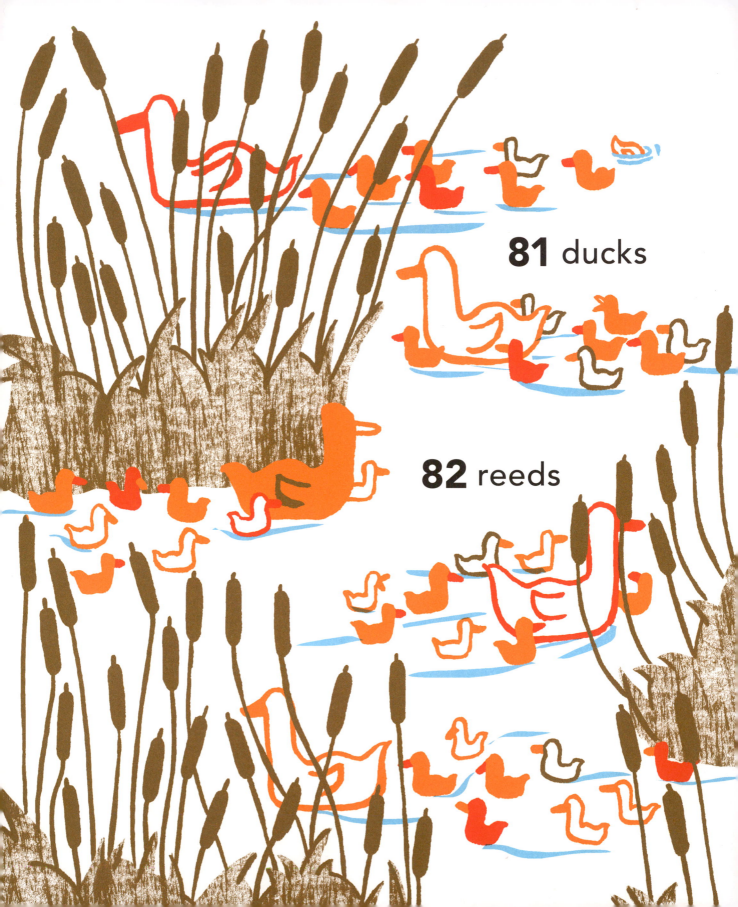

81 ducks

82 reeds

glides on the water

84 flags

85 floats on the water

86 dries on the line

87 birds

On a wall made
of **88** bricks

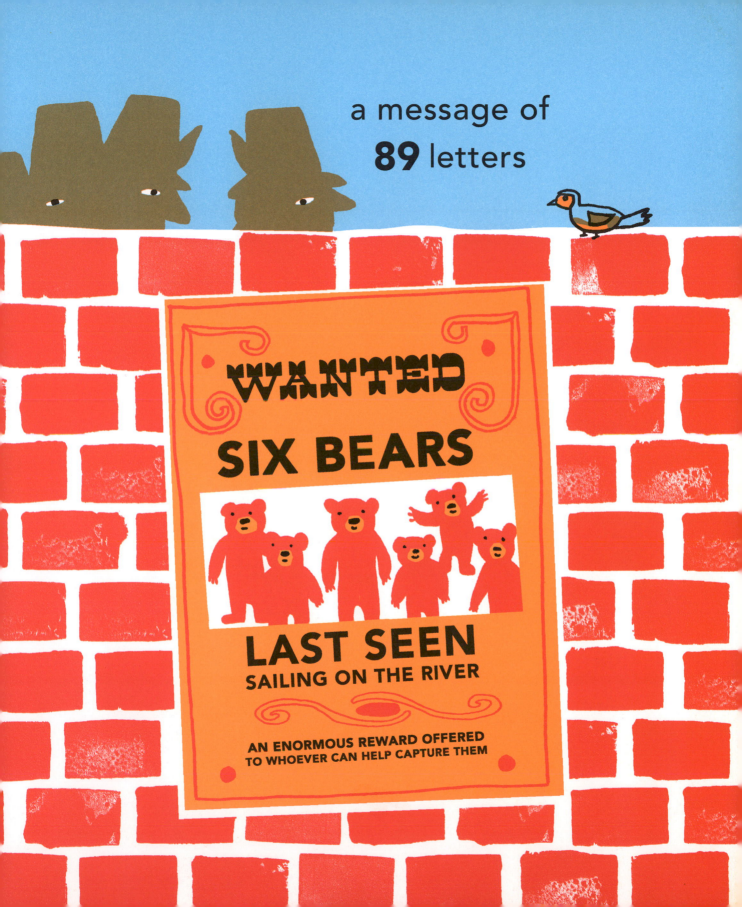

90 bees lead the hunters to the bears

Everyone makes peace with **91** slices of gingerbread and **92** sugar pearls

In this bonkers bear tale...
the dirtiest bear has **93** fleas

The strongest one can carry up to

94 kilos

The shortest one
is only **95** cm

The greediest one can eat up to
97 blueberries in one sitting

The most athletic one
wears shirt number

99 stones to find your way home

100 trees...

The forest